SlowPoke

by Lucille Recht Penner
Illustrated by Gioia Fiammenghi

The Kane Press
New York

Book Design/Art Direction: Roberta Pressel

Library of Congress Cataloging-in-Publication Data

Penner, Lucille Recht.
    Slowpoke / by Lucille Recht Penner ; illustrated by Gioia Fiammenghi.
        p.   cm. — (Math matters.)
    Summary: Tired of everyone calling him slow, Teddy practices his running and keeps track of the time it takes to run to the school bus or the store as he prepares to run a big race.
    ISBN 1-57565-108-4 (pbk. : alk. paper)
    [1. Time measurements—Fiction. 2. Running—Fiction. 3. Running races—Fiction.]
    I. Fiammenghi, Gioia, ill. II. Title. III. Series.
PZ7.P38465 Sl 2001
[Fic]—dc21

2001000880

10 9 8 7 6 5 4 3 2 1

First published in the United States of America in 2001 by The Kane Press.
Printed in Hong Kong.

MATH MATTERS is a registered trademark of The Kane Press.

Teddy Kramer wasn't very fast. His dad could run much faster. His mother could too. His brother, Joe—forget it! All Teddy ever saw were the bottoms of Joe's shoes disappearing around the corner.

The other kids called Teddy "Slowpoke."
Even his best friend, Robert, called him
"Slowpoke."

Teddy was always the last kid on line.

He always got tagged out.

At the beach Teddy was always the
last one in the water.

Teddy was never first at anything.

One day Teddy's class went to the zoo. Teddy was last on the bus, so he had to sit next to a teacher—Mr. Stone.

After they saw the snakes and the penguins, everybody went for ice cream. Teddy was last again. They were out of his favorite flavor, Frooti Tooti.

Then the class hurried to line up for the petting zoo. Teddy was the last one to get to feed the animals. They weren't hungry anymore.

It was a terrible day.

"I'm sick of being a slowpoke," Teddy
told Robert when they got back to school.
"Why don't you try to get faster?" said
Robert. "Practice running every day. And,
really concentrate—no daydreaming!"
"Okay, I'll think about it." Teddy said.

He told his family about Robert's idea.

"I know you can do it," said his mom.

"The problem is," his brother Joe said, "you're always slowing down and looking around."

"Dawdling," said his father. "Try to concentrate on getting where you're going."

Hmmm, thought Teddy.

On Monday Teddy ran from his house to the bus stop.

On the way he waved to the tree doctor.

He picked up a quarter lying on the street.

He petted a big white dog.

It took him six minutes. He was last on the bus—as usual.

START
8:00

FINISH
8:06

Teddy was last on Tuesday and Wednesday, too. On Thursday he left late. He really had to rush—or miss the bus. He was panting when he got there. "I made it in four minutes!" he told Robert. "Two minutes faster than usual."

"Wow, how come?" Robert asked.

"I was late, so I didn't dawdle," said Teddy. "Not for a second."

When they got off the bus, Teddy ran into school. A teacher stopped him. It was Mr. Stone.

"No running here," Mr. Stone said. "Slow down."

Ha! That was the first time anyone ever said that to Teddy.

He liked it.

START
8:02

FINISH
8:06

Teddy decided to run whenever he could. Every afternoon he ran up and down the block five times. It took him twenty minutes.

Steven and Sara called to him, "We made cookies. Do you want one?"

"Yes," Teddy said. "But I can't stop."

Steven ran up and gave him a cookie.

"Thanks," Teddy said. "I love banana chip cookies!" He kept on running.

He didn't stop to look at the new baby triplets.

He didn't even stop when a fire engine pulled into Mr. Lee's driveway.

On Saturday his mom needed something at the Quick Mart, so Teddy ran to get it.

It used to take Teddy 20 minutes to get to the store. Now he could run there in 12 minutes. He used the extra eight minutes to look at *Runner* magazine.

START
11:10

FINISH
11:22

On the way home Teddy ran into Joe.

"Are you practicing for the race?" Joe asked him.

Teddy stopped short. "What race?"

"You know—to raise money for the library," Joe said. "Mom signed up both of us."

I'm in a race! Teddy thought. He gulped.
"Suppose I come in last?" he asked Joe.

"Don't worry," said Joe. "It's finishing the
race that counts."

But I don't want to be *last*, Teddy
thought. I've got to practice even more.

Recess was 40 minutes long. Some kids
played ball. Others climbed the monkey bars.
Teddy didn't play. He ran. He ran so fast, the
trees were a blur. He ran for 25 minutes.

"Whew!" said Teddy. That's it for now."

START
11:50

FINISH
12:15

Teddy stopped at the water fountain. A teacher came up to him. It was Mr. Stone— again. Uh-oh.

But Mr. Stone wasn't mad. "You're fast," he said.

Maybe it's true, Teddy thought. Maybe I *am* fast. Maybe I can even win the race if I try very hard...if I practice and concentrate.

Teddy's schedule
Run ☺ 4:00 – 4:30
Homework ☹
       5:00 – 5:40
Dinner ☺ 5:45 – 6:20
Run ☺ 6:30
until Tired

He used to run for 20 minutes every day after school. Now he ran for 30 minutes.

He concentrated so hard he finished all his homework in 40 minutes.

Teddy ate dinner in 35 minutes—and he didn't get a single spot on his napkin!

After dinner he ran some more. He even ran backwards!

He didn't come in until his mom called—twice!

Finally—it was race day! Teddy's group lined up. Teddy (number 5) was next to Peter Jack (number 4). He was the fastest runner around.

Teddy looked over. Peter Jack was tying his shoelaces for the third time! Was he nervous?

Teddy retied his own shoelaces. "Maybe I can win," he said to himself. "I'm sure going to try!"

He crouched down and waited for the whistle.

When the whistle blew, Teddy leaped
forward. He passed some kids but there
were still plenty in front of him.

He ran faster. Only three kids were
ahead of him now.

"Concentrate!" Teddy told himself.
He was gaining on Peter Jack.

Peter Jack pulled ahead. Then Teddy
pulled ahead. They were almost side by
side.

Then Teddy crossed the finish line.
He had won the race!

Teddy's family ran up to him. Robert was right behind them.

"Congratulations!" everyone shouted.

"You were very fast," his mom said.

"All that practice sure paid off!" his dad added.

"You concentrated!" Robert told him.

"You're awesome," said Joe.

"Me?" said Teddy. "Wow!"

Guess what? No one called Teddy "Slowpoke" after that.

He had a new nickname—"Slow down!"

ELAPSED TIME CHART

> ELAPSED TIME is the amount of time that passes between a START TIME and a FINISH TIME.

Can you find Joe's FINISH TIME?

Hint: Count forward 40 minutes from 2:40.

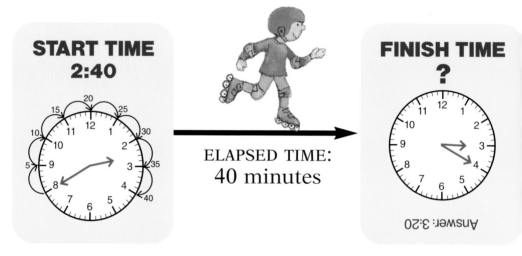

START TIME
2:40

ELAPSED TIME:
40 minutes

FINISH TIME
?

Answer: 3:20

Can you find Teddy's ELAPSED TIME?

Hint: Count forward until you get to 4:40.

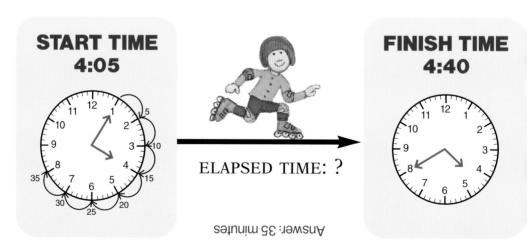

START TIME
4:05

ELAPSED TIME: ?

FINISH TIME
4:40

Answer: 35 minutes